Storybook

Collection

First published by Parragon in 2013
Parragon
Chartist House
15-17 Trim Street
Bath BA1 1HA, UK
www.parragon.com

ISBN 978-1-4723-0815-3

Printed in China

Storybook
Collection

Bath · New York · Singapore · Hong Kong · Cologne · Delhi
Melbourne · Amsterdam · Johannesburg · Shenzhen

Contents

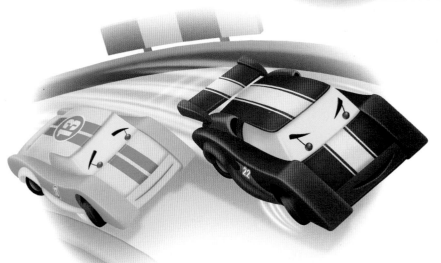

Space
Adventure

Welcome to Adventure Day at the Mickey Mouse Clubhouse! Mickey and the gang have a treasure map from Professor Von Drake. They're going to the moon, to Mars, to Saturn – and to a mystery planet – to find a treasure!

Space Captain Mickey says, "Let's go, space adventurers!"

"Not so fast!" says the Professor. He explains that along the way, Mickey and the gang must find ten Treasure Stars. These stars will lead them to the mystery planet – and to the treasure!

Everyone is on board – even Toodles. They count down:

ten, nine, eight, seven, six, five, four, three, two, one ...

Blast off!

The gang doesn't know that someone is spying on them!

It's Space Pirate Pete! "Arrgh!" he says. "That space treasure will be mine!"

Pete has a new helper named Quoodles. He asks her for a tool to stop Mickey's ship. Quoodles has a milk carton.

"What good is a milk carton?" asks Pete. "Oh, I get it. All those milk cartons will block the rocket!"

"Look at all that milk," says Goofy. "This must be the Milky Way!"

Space Pirate Pete says,

"You're surrounded by milk.

Give up the treasure map!"

"No way!" says Mickey.

"We need a Mouseketool.

Oh, Toodles!"

But Toodles doesn't show

up. Where is he?

15

Toodles sees Quoodles outside the ship. Toodles has never seen anyone else who looks like him! They smile at each other and make silly faces.

"Oh, TOODLES!" calls Mickey.

Toodles hears Mickey. He waves goodbye to Quoodles.

Toodles brings a Mouseketool. It's a giant cookie! The cookie floats away and the milk cartons follow it into space.

"Oh, space sticks!" says Space Pirate Pete. "Foiled again!"

Minnie giggles. "Everyone knows milk goes with cookies."

On the Moon, Mickey meets Moon-Man Chip and Moon-Man Dale. Mickey asks if they have seen any Treasure Stars.

"We see lots of space junk," they say. "We put it all in our Moon Locker."

"Then take us to your locker!" says Space Captain Mickey.

Moon-Men Chip and Dale lead

them to their locker. Goofy opens it.

"I think they need a bigger locker," says Goofy.

Hot dog! There are Treasure Stars one, two and three!

The Treasure Stars fly to the spaceship and stick on like magic!

"Now we're ready to go to our next stop," says Mickey.

"Mars, here we come!"

On Mars, Mickey meets Martian Mickey – and Pluto from Pluto!

Mickey asks Martian Mickey if he knows where to find any Treasure Stars.

22

Martian Mickey says, "They may be in the Star Tree Forest!"

23

Meanwhile, back at the ship, Toodles sees Quoodles again.

He gives her some flowers.

But Pirate Pete stops by. "Quoodles," he says, "stop your

dillydallyin'. We gotta get that treasure map!"

Quoodles has to go. Poor Toodles!

Martian Mickey takes the gang to the Star Tree Forest.
"We don't have many trees on Mars, so every tree is a
forest," he says.

Stars four, five and six are on the tree. They fly off and
go straight to the rocket ship.

Space Pirate Pete has another trick up his sleeve.

He pretends to be a little old lady who is lost in space.

The little old lady asks Goofy for a map.

"Goofy, nooooo!" says Donald.

But it's too late. Goofy gives Pete the treasure map!

Goofy sure goofed. They've got to get the map back! Mickey, Goofy and Donald chase Pete around the rings of Saturn, but they can't catch that tricky space pirate. Then Mickey falls off the rings and floats away into outer space. Oh, no!

Mickey bumps into space rocks until Pluto rescues him.

"Thanks, Pluto," says Mickey.

Pluto and Mickey fly back to Saturn and the ship.

On the way, they find the last Treasure Stars: seven,

eight, nine and ten!

Back on Saturn, Toodles brings a Mouseketool – a big birdcage – to trap Pete. Donald grabs the map!

But then Quoodles brings one of her tools. It's a Space Chicken to help Pete get away!

Now Mickey and his crew have the map and all ten Treasure Stars. The stars light the way to the mystery planet.

"Hey, that planet looks familiar," says Goofy. "Let's call it Planet Mickey!"

The stars shine on the X that marks the spot.

And it's off to Planet Mickey to find the treasure!

Uh-oh. Space Pirate Pete gets to Planet Mickey

first and finds the X that marks the treasure spot.

Pete has one last trick. He throws out a sticky web.

"Now when those little space adventurers try to pass through

here and get the treasure, they'll get stuck!" says Pete.

But it's Quoodles who gets stuck in the web.

"Poor Quoodles," says Pete. "I gotta rescue you!"

"Help!" yells Pete. "Somebody HELP!"

Mickey hears him and comes right away.

33

But now Toodles gets stuck in the sticky web, too!

"What can we do?" asks Pete.

Mickey says, "I'm going to use a Mouseketool!"

"That's a great idea," says Pete. "And I'll use a

Quoodles tool!"

Even though he is stuck, Toodles sends Mickey a Mouseketool. It is ... Space Pirate Pete! And Quoodles' tool is ... Mickey the Space Captain Mouse!

"What can it mean?" asks Pete.

"It means we can save Toodles and Quoodles if we work together as friends!" says Mickey.

Mickey and Pete jump up and down on the arch holding the web. The arch breaks. Toodles and Quoodles are free!

Wheeee!

Everyone is happy to meet Quoodles – and to see that Pete has given up his 'piratey' ways. Pluto points to the X. He knows where to dig. Pluto digs up the treasure chest. Inside is Professor Von Drake's remote control. Minnie says, "Push the button, Mickey!"

The ground shakes and up comes …

... the Mickey Mouse Space House! What a terrific treasure!

Martian Mickey says, "Now when you visit us, you'll have a fun place to play."

"Hot dog!" says Mickey.

Everyone does the out-of-this-world Hot Dog Dance!

38

39

As Mickey and the gang head back to their

Clubhouse on Earth, Martian Mickey waves.

"Thanks for stopping by!"

Jake
and the
Spyglass

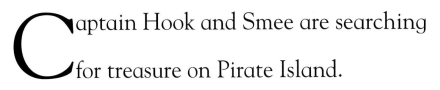

Captain Hook and Smee are searching for treasure on Pirate Island.

"**Blast it**, Smee! There's nothing but seashells on this seashore," says Captain Hook. "Where is all the treasure?"

"Oh, these pretty shells are a treasure of their own," says Smee. "Don't you think so, Cap'n?"

Just then, Captain Hook notices something shiny in the water.

"Look alive, Smee," says Hook. "There's treasure out there on the water! Give me my spyglass."

"Oh, dear," says Smee. "I'm afraid I ... I don't have your spyglass, Cap'n."

"You lost my spyglass?" asks Captain Hook.

"It would seem so, sir," says Smee. "But don't worry, Cap'n. We can row out in the dinghy and see what that shiny thing is for ourselves."

"I have a better idea," says Hook. "We can row out in the dinghy and see what that shiny thing is for ourselves."

"It's this way," they each say, pointing in opposite directions.

"Without that spyglass," says Hook, "we can't see where we left the dinghy."

44

On another part of the beach, Izzy, Cubby and Skully are collecting seashells.

"Wow, the tide sure brought in a lot of shells," says Izzy.

"They're so pretty," says Cubby.

"I wonder what else might wash in with the tide?" Jake says.

"I'm gonna take a look with my trusty spyglass."

"**Whew,**" says Cubby. "It's getting hot."

"Yeah, really hot!" agrees Izzy. "I know!

Why don't we go swimming and cool off?"

"Great idea, Iz," says Jake.

"Yay-hey, let's play," says Izzy.

"Last one in is a rusty anchor!" says Jake.

"Wait for me!" calls Cubby.

"Why is it so hot on this infernal beach?" asks Hook.

"We could always take a little swim, Cap'n," suggests Smee.

"I don't want a little swim," says Hook. "I want to find the dinghy and go get that treasure!"

Just then, Captain Hook hears something.

Splish, splash!

"Do you see what I see, Smee?" asks Hook.

"Oh, yes, Cap'n," says Smee. "Those sea pups are having such fun splashing around! Please, can we go for a dip?"

"No," says Hook. "It's Jake's spyglass on that towel. Quick! Hide before they see us!"

"But, Cap'n," says Smee, "if we ask the sea pups nicely, maybe we can borrow their spyglass to find our dinghy."

"Why borrow the spyglass when we can take it?" says Hook. He uses his fishing hook to try and nab the spyglass.

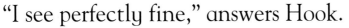

"Can you see without your spyglass, Cap'n?" asks Smee.

"I see perfectly fine," answers Hook.

Yoink! Oops! Hook nabs a rubber ring instead.

"Good thinking, sir," says Smee.

"That'll come in handy when we

find the dinghy."

Hook tries again. Yoink! This time he grabs a seashell.

"Not a spyglass, sir," says Smee. "But it is beautiful."

"Ouch!" yells Hook as a hermit crab comes out of the shell and pinches his nose.

"Blast and barnacles! We're going to have to do this the old-fashioned way," says Hook. "Run!"

Hook runs onto the beach and grabs the spyglass.

"Crackers!" says Skully. "That not-so-sneaky snook just ran off with our spyglass!"

"Which way did he go?" asks Cubby.

"I don't know," says Jake. "Without our spyglass, we can't see that far!"

"Leave it to me," says Skully. He flies up high in the air and spots Hook and Smee getting into their dinghy.

"Dinghy, ahoy!"

calls Skully. "That-a-way!"

"Hurry, mateys, into the

rowboat," says Jake. "We'll catch

them in the water!"

"Heave-ho!" calls Jake.

"It's no use," says Cubby. "We can't paddle in this strong wind!"

"I've got an idea," says Izzy. "Give me those towels!"

Izzy ties the towels together to make a sail!

"We'll ride the wind right over to those pirates!" says Izzy.

"It's working," says Cubby.

"Awesome," says Jake. "We'll catch that dinghy in no time!"

"Smee, you slowcoach, can't we go any faster?"

asks Captain Hook.

"Sorry – ugh – Cap'n," says Smee. "This wind is blowin' mighty hard. Maybe we'd go faster if you helped me row?"

"Help you row?" says Hook. "You just need to work harder. Put your back into it! We're almost at the shiny thing!"

"Aye-ugh-aye, Cap'n," says Smee.

"Well, hello, Captain," says Jake.

"I think you have something that belongs to us!"

"We'll be taking that spyglass back now," says Skully.

"I hope you find what you're looking for," says Cubby.

Hook is surprised. But then he remembers the shiny thing.

"Who needs their spyglass when there is treasure upon us!"

"Look, Cap'n, it's your spyglass!" says Smee.

"At least something has gone my way today!" says Hook.

Hook looks through the spyglass and sees . . . a giant eye!

"Smee, what is that?" asks Hook.

"Uh, Cap'n, we best get going now," says Smee.

Hook finds himself face-to-face with the Tick Tock Croc!

"Smee, what are you waiting for? Row!" yells Hook,

dropping the spyglass.

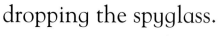

Tick tock, tick tock.

The Croc chases the dinghy

out to sea.

"Whoa!" says Izzy. "It looks like Hook might never see his spyglass again!"

"That's too bad," says Jake. "If Hook had just asked us if he could borrow our spyglass, we could've helped him."

"It's like you always say, Jake," says Cubby. "You should ask permission before you borrow something that isn't yours."

"I hope that sneaky snook learns his lesson," says Skully.

"Let's head back to Pirate Island," says Jake.

"For solving pirate problems today, we earned Gold Doubloons," says Jake.

"What are we waiting for?" asks Izzy. "Let's open up the team treasure chest and count them!"

"Cool," says Cubby.

"We earned nine Gold Doubloons," says Jake.

"Yay-hey, well done, crew," says Izzy.

To Play
Another Day

At U.N.I.Q.U.E. headquarters, Special Agent Oso prepares for his fitness test. "I'm ready, Wolfie," he says.

"The wires connect to the computer that will tell us how fit you are," says Special Agent Wolfie.

"I already know I'm as fit as a fiddle," says Oso. "I exercise every day."

"Exercise keeps an agent alert," says Wolfie.

"And exercise builds healthy bones and muscles," Oso adds.

"Right, but you have to stick with it," Wolfie says. "Just like this test, Oso. You have to stick with it all the way to the end."

"Whoa!" says Agent Oso. "This thing is fast!"

"Keep going until the green light turns red," Wolfie says. "Good luck, Oso!"

In a nearby neighbourhood, Enzio's mother asks, "Enzio, how long have you been sitting in front of the TV?"

"I'm not sure," he says. "Since I stopped playing computer games, I guess."

"We need to get you up and moving more," Enzio's mum says.

"What should I do?" asks Enzio.

"I want you to think of ways you can get more exercise. And I'd like you to tell me your ideas before suppertime."

"But I don't know how to get more exercise," says Enzio.

Hovering far above the Earth, the Tracking Satellite sees that Enzio needs help. The satellite sends an emergency message to headquarters.

79

"This fitness test is a real workout!" Oso says. "I'd like to stop, but Wolfie said something about 'sticking to it'. I wonder what he meant?"

Paw Pilot receives the signal from the Tracking Satellite. "Special alert! Special alert!" she shouts.

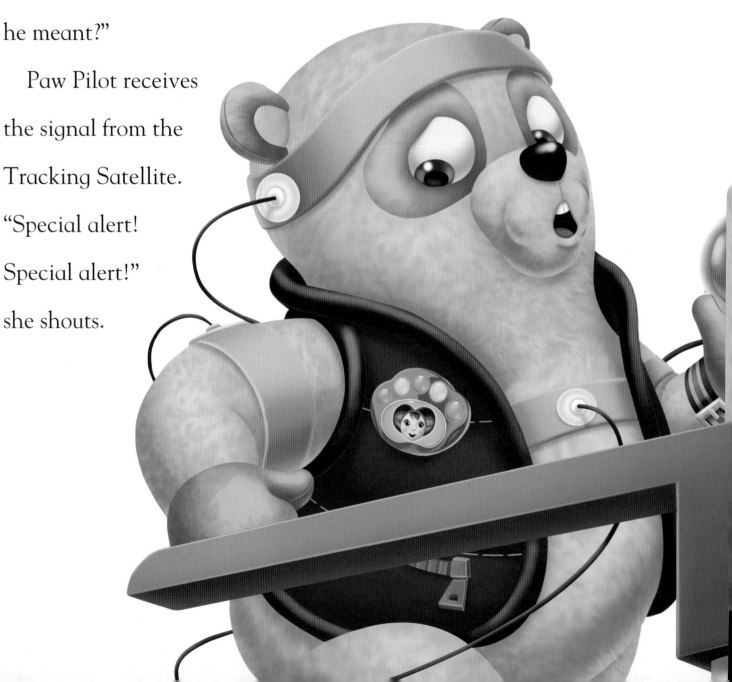

Whoops! Agent Oso misses a step and tumbles off the treadmill.

"Agent Oso!" says Mister Dos. "I have a special assignment for you."

"Enzio must find ways to exercise," says Mister Dos. "He needs your help!"

"Special assignment accepted!" says Oso.

"Hurry, Oso," says Mister Dos. "Enzio's mother wants to hear his plan by suppertime!"

"It looks like Enzio's house isn't far," replies Oso. "I'll jog over."

"Enzio's house wasn't as close as I thought," Oso says.

"There's no time to lose," Paw Pilot reminds him. "I'm ready with your three special steps."

"Hello Agent Oso," says Enzio. "What are you doing here?"

"I'm going to help you plan how to get more exercise, Enzio," Oso says. "What's the first step, Paw Pilot?"

"Step one: find activities that interest you," says Paw Pilot.

"Okay, Enzio. So what do you like to do?" asks Agent Oso.

"I like playing computer games and watching TV," says Enzio.

"But you won't get any exercise that way," says Oso.

"Your body wants to move," Oso tells Enzio. "To be healthy, you need to excercise for at least an hour every day."

"What can I do?" says Enzio.

"There is a park across the street," Oso says. "Let's see what other kids are doing."

87

"I see a girl riding her bike," says Enzio. "And a lady walking her dog. Some kids are playing tag, too."

"Right!" says Oso. "I also see a girl on a skateboard and some kids playing basketball."

"I'd like to play basketball!" Enzio says.

89

"Agent Oso! Are you on a special assignment?" asks one of the basketball players.

"Yes!" says Oso. "Would you mind if I show Enzio some basketball basics?"

"Okay!" says the girl.

"When you play basketball, you bounce the ball," says Oso.

"That's called dribbling," adds the girl.

"I can do that," says Enzio.

"Great. Now, watch me," says Agent Oso. "I'm going to dribble, jump up and shoot the ball into the basket."

"Be careful, Oso!" yells Enzio.

"It's all part of the plan," says Oso. "More or less."

Enzio smiles. "I like basketball. I'll ask my mum if I can join a team."

"Sign ups end next week," says the girl. "You could be on my team."

"Step one is complete," says Paw Pilot.

93

"What's the next step, Paw Pilot?" Oso asks.

"Step two is to plan to play at least one hour every day," says Paw Pilot.

"Being on a sports team will take care of some days, Enzio," says Agent Oso. "But what about the other days?"

"I can ride my bike," says Enzio. "Or play tag in the park!"

"Step two is complete," says Paw Pilot. "Step three is to stick with it!"

"Hey! That's what Wolfie told me to do. 'Stick with it'," Agent Oso says.

"You will always need to exercise," says Paw Pilot.

"I'll ask my mum to help me stick with the plan," promises Enzio.

"Agent Oso has been helping me come up with an excercise plan," says Enzio. "I'd like to join a basketball team, Mama. And I'll ride my bike and play tag in the park."

"Those are wonderful ideas, dear," she says.

"Well done, Oso," says Paw Pilot. "Your special assignment was a success!"

"Just doing my job!" says Oso. "Now if you'll excuse me, I have a fitness test to stick to!"

"Thank you, Oso!" calls Enzio. "Goodbye!"

97

"Wolfie said to stick with the fitness test until the light turns red," says Oso. "It's not easy, but I know I can do it!"

"I did it!" shouts Agent Oso. "I completed the test!"

"Owwwt-standing," says Wolfie. "The computer has confirmed

that you are indeed fit as a fiddle."

"Congratulations, Agent Oso," says Paw Pilot. "You have earned your fitness test award."

Suddenly, Agent Oso's watch pops open. "That's not all," says Mister Dos. "By helping Enzio come up with a plan he could stick to, you have earned a staying fit digi medal."

"Thanks, Mister Dos," Oso says. "This fitness mission fits me perfectly!"

This digi medal is for you!

Toadhog Trouble

Ellyvan and Zooter are playing catch.
Suddenly, they hear something....

"Does not!" says Bungo.

"Does, too!" says Toadhog.

Oh, no! Toadhog and Bungo are fighting!

Toadhog got lost going to the mud pond!

"This sign points to the mud pond!"

says Toadhog.

"It does not," says

Bungo. "That sign is for the

Coconut Grove."

107

"Bungo, your signs are silly!" shouts Toadhog. Bungo takes his sign and rolls away.

"Toadhog!" says Zooter. "That wasn't very nice.

You hurt Bungo's feelings."

"Maybe you should say you're sorry," says Ellyvan.

"Harrumph!" says Toadhog.

Oh, no! Bungo is so upset that he takes down all his signs!

Taxicrab is going
to the banana tree.

But without seeing a sign, he doesn't know where to go!

Not that way!

Splash!

Hippobus is
driving the Beetle
Bugs to school.
Hmm, which way
do I go? she wonders.

"I don't need Bungo's silly signs," says Toadhog. "I can find the mud pond myself."

Not that way! Buzzzz!

"Have you seen Hippobus?" asks Miss Jolly. "The Beetle Bugs are not at school!"

"Which way to the banana tree?" asks Taxicrab. "I can't make smoothies without bananas!"

Suddenly, Toadhog races by.
He's being chased by a swarm
of bees!

"Ahh!"
cries Toadhog.

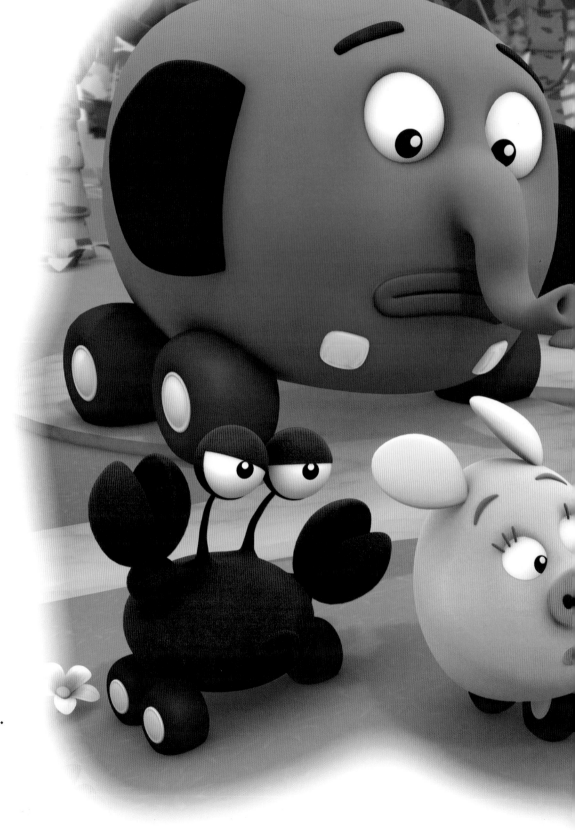

"Oh, dear," says
Zooter. "We need
Bungo's signs!"
"Toadhog, you
have to apologize to
Bungo," says Ellyvan.

124

"All right, all right," says Toadhog.

125

Zooter, Ellyvan and Toadhog go to Bungo's warren.

"Bungo, you make the best signs in Jungle Junction," says Toadhog. "And ... I got lost without them. I'm sorry."

"Well, okay," Bungo says with a smile.

Toadhog helps Bungo
put back all the signs.
Hippobus brings the
Beetle Bugs to school.

Taxicrab picks loads of bananas!

"Smoothies for everyone!" he says.

And as the sun sets on Jungle Junction, two friends

enjoy banana smoothies and a nice mud bath.

Rundown Race Car

Doc and Donny are getting ready to race.

Donny puts Ricardo Race Car at the starting line.

Doc picks up a yellow race car and puts it next to Ricardo.

"After Ricardo beats your car, he's going to be ready

for the Championship-Best-Race-Car-Ever race!" Donny says.

"Let's get this race going," Doc says to her brother with a smile.

The racers start their engines ... and they're off!

136

Ricardo takes the lead.

Donny and Doc watch as the cars zoom around the track.

"Only one more lap to go before Ricardo wins the race!"

Donny cheers.

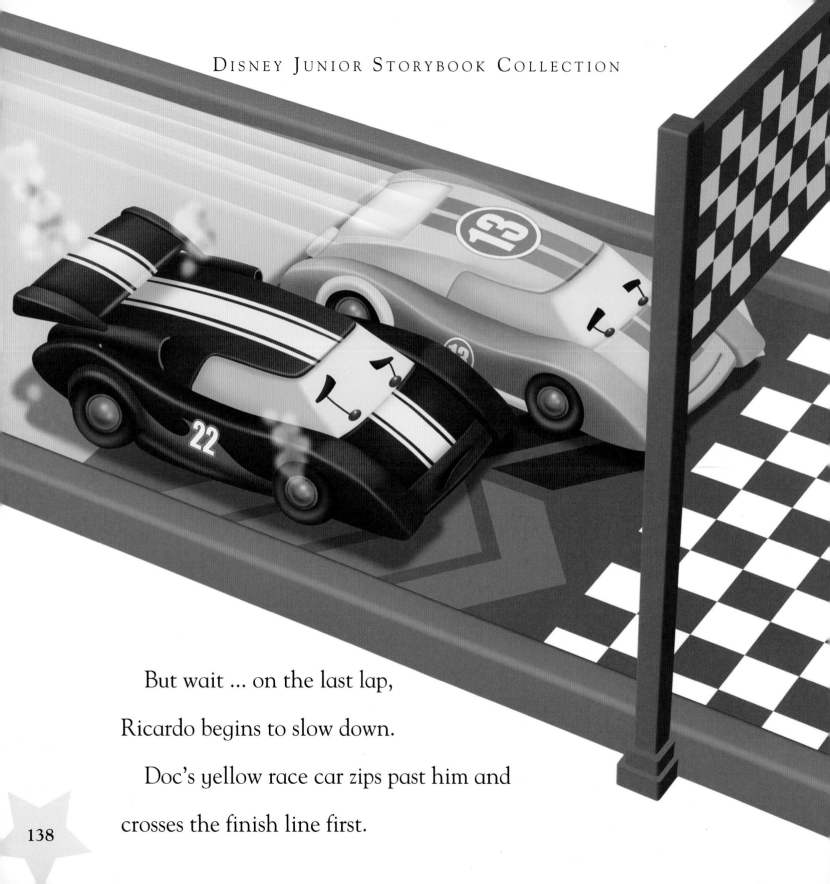

But wait ... on the last lap,

Ricardo begins to slow down.

Doc's yellow race car zips past him and

crosses the finish line first.

138

"You won!" Donny yells. "That's not possible!"

Donny's eyes fill with tears. He throws the

remote control to the floor.

"I'm sorry, Donny," says Doc.

Dad comes in to see what's wrong.

"Donny, I think you need a nap," Dad says.

"But I'm not tired," Donny says. Then he yawns.

"Why don't I see if I can fix Ricardo?" Doc says.

"Good idea, Doc," says Dad.

Dad steers Donny to his bedroom.

"If you get some sleep now, it will recharge your batteries," Dad says.

142

"I'll fix Ricardo before your friend Luca gets here for the big race," Doc adds.

Doc carries Ricardo to her clinic while Donny naps.

Her stethoscope begins to glow.

Then magically, all the toys come to life.

Stuffy sees what Doc has in her hand.

"Ricardo Race Car?" says Stuffy. "I'm his number one fan!"

Ricardo wonders why he is being carried.

He's the greatest race car there is. Surely he

can race his way across a garden!

"You haven't been going as fast as usual," Doc explains.

"I'm worried something might be wrong with you."

Ricardo doesn't know what Doc is talking about.

He is faster than any race car around!

But when Doc puts him on the ground, he

sputters and stops.

"But I have a big race today," Ricardo moans.

"Donny's counting on me!"

It's time for Doc to give Ricardo a checkup.

She lifts his bonnet and looks at his engine.

Everything looks okay in there.

"Can you give me a big *vroom vroom?*" Doc asks.

Ricardo tries, but his vroom doesn't have a lot of power behind it.

Hallie thinks Ricardo looks worn out.

"You raced a billion times last night, right?" Doc asks.

"Yes, this is true," says Ricardo. "A billion times exactly."

Doc knows what is wrong.

"My diagnosis is No-*Vroom-Vroom*-atosis!" she tells Ricardo.

Ricardo needs to recharge his battery!

Doc asks Dad to plug Ricardo into the charger.

Before long, Ricardo's battery light turns green.

By the time Donny's nap is over, Ricardo will be all revved up.

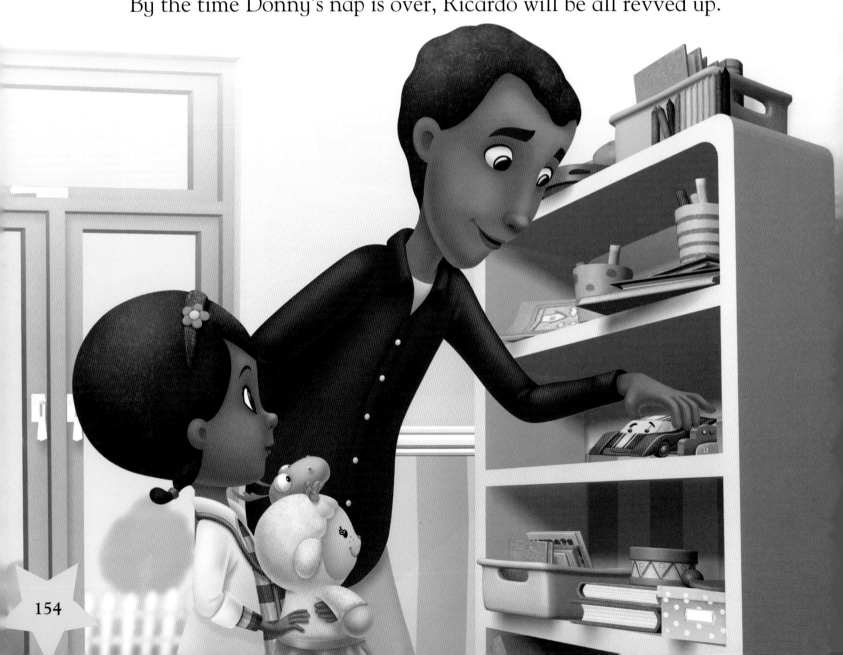

Later on, Donny's friend Luca comes over to play.

Donny puts Ricardo Race Car at the starting line.

Luca picks up his car and puts it next to Ricardo.

The racers start their engines ... and they're off!

155

On the last lap, Ricardo begins to speed up.

"Go, Ricardo! Go!" Doc cheers.

He zips past Luca's car and crosses the finish line. Ricardo wins!

"Thanks, Doc!" says Donny. "You're the best big sister in the whole wide world!"

The End